LITTLE REDHEAD,
Did you know?

By William Sheerin
Illustrated by Michael Rausch

THIS BOOK IS DEDICATED TO MY TWO GINGERS, BRENNAN AND TOBY.
MAY YOUR FUTURES BE AS BRIGHT AS THE HAIRS ON YOUR HEAD.
-DAD

LITTLE REDHEAD, DID YOU KNOW

LITTLE REDHEAD, ARE YOU AWARE
that a mutation causes your red hair?
Like a ninja llama, you are unique.

LITTLE REDHEAD,
DO YOU HAVE A CLUE
if what they say is really true,
that a kiss from the sun
is a freckle on you?

Oh it must be a ton of fun
to get kisses from the sun.

HE LOVES YOU more than *anyone*.

LITTLE REDHEAD, DID YOU HEAR?
You have your very own day of the year?
and not just *one*,
but *two*,

WE ♥ REDHEADS

HAPPY Redhea

not for
    green hair,
            blonde
        or blue,
But this special day's just for you.

So go ahead and clap your hands
and celebrate those red strands
JUST LIKE THEY DO IN THE NETHERLANDS

LITTLE REDHEAD, did you hear about this ginger drought?

Statistics shout,
"WE'RE RUNNING OUT!"

But now's no time to *panic!*

to the Atlantic

CALLING
ALL
GINGERS

near and far.

Redheads can be

BIG

or small.

some
are short,

and
some
are
tall.

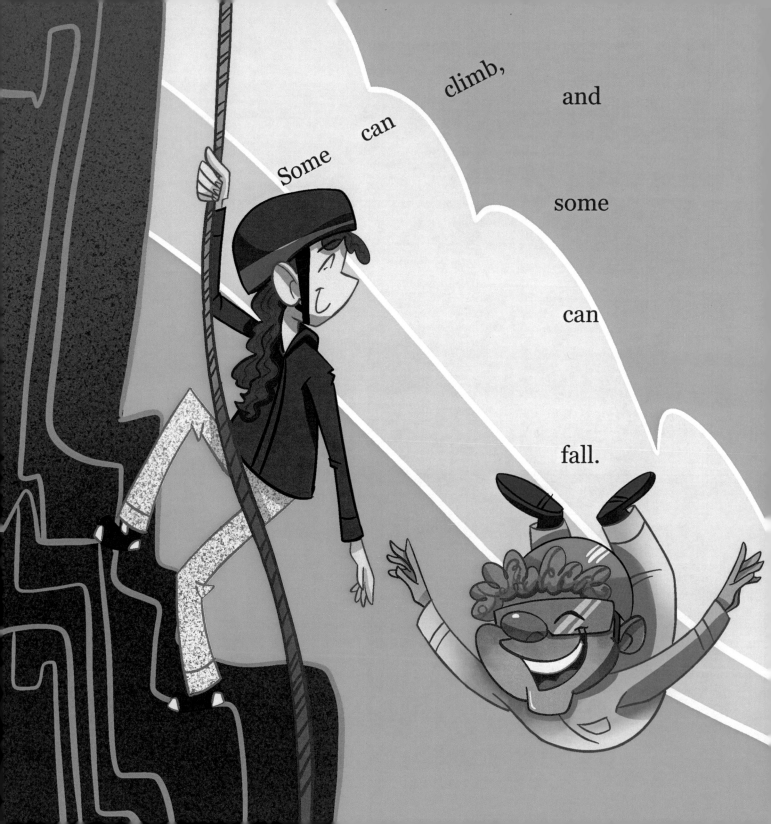

Some are timid,

AND

SOME

DO

BRAWL.

But mostly,

there aren't many redheads

at all.

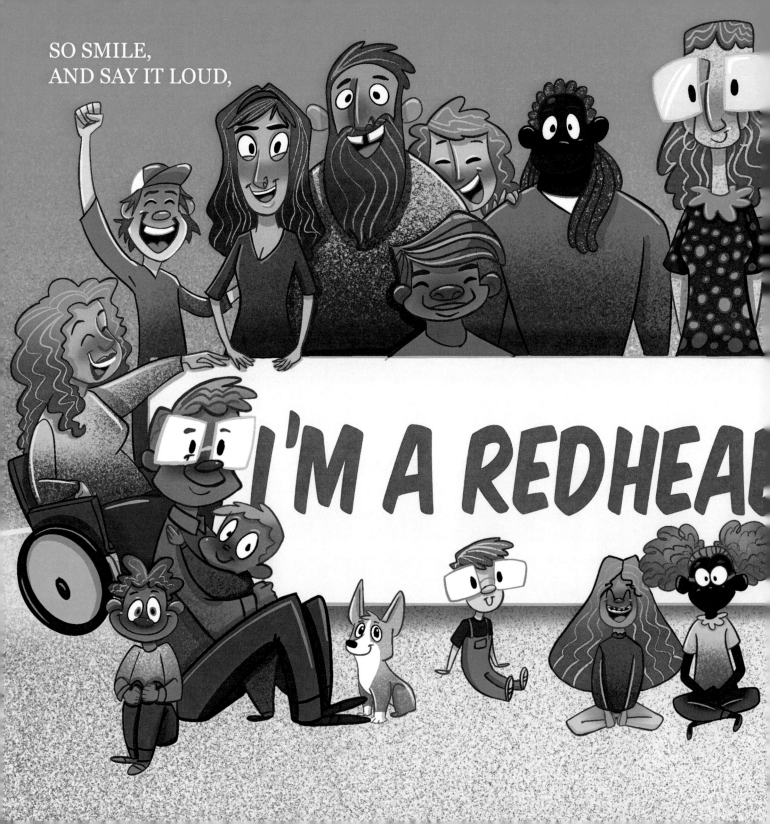

SO SMILE,
AND SAY IT LOUD,

I'M A REDHEAD

Because this much is true,
God made it all through and through,

He just made a little less of you.

Made in United States
North Haven, CT
11 November 2023